First U.S. edition 2006

Library of Congress Cataloging-in-Publication Data

Browne, Anthony, date.
Silly Billy / Anthony Browne. — 1st U.S. ed.
p.   cm.
Summary: To help with his anxiety, Bllly uses the worry dolls his grandmother
recommends, but he finds that they do not quite solve his problem
ISBN-10 0-7636-3124-8
ISBN-13 978-0-7636-3124-6
[1. Worry—Fiction. 2. Dolls—Fiction.] I. Title.
PZ7.B81984Sil 2006
[E]—dc22   2005055305

2 4 6 8 10 9 7 5 3

Printed in China

This book was typeset in Futura.
The illustrations were done in watercolor and colored pencil.

Candlewick Press
2067 Massachusetts Avenue
Cambridge, Massachusetts 02140

visit us at www.candlewick.com

SILLY BILLY

Anthony Browne

CANDLEWICK PRESS
CAMBRIDGE, MASSACHUSETTS

Billy used to be
a bit of a worrier.

He
worried
about
many things....

Billy worried about **hats**,

and he worried about **shoes**.

Billy worried about **clouds**

and **rain**.

Billy even worried about **giant birds**.

His dad tried to help.
"Don't worry, son," he said.
"None of those things could happen.
It's just your imagination."

His mom tried too.
"Don't worry, darling," she said.
"We won't let anything
hurt you."

But Billy still worried.

One night he had to
stay with his grandma.
But Billy couldn't sleep.
He was too worried.
He always worried
about staying at other
people's houses.
Billy felt a little silly,
but at last he got up
and went to tell
his grandma.

"Well, my goodness, dear," she said. "You're not silly. When I was your age, I used to worry like that. I've got just the thing for you."

She went into her room and came
out holding something.
"These are worry dolls," she explained.
"Just tell each of them one of your worries
and put them under your pillow. They'll do
all the worrying for you while you sleep."

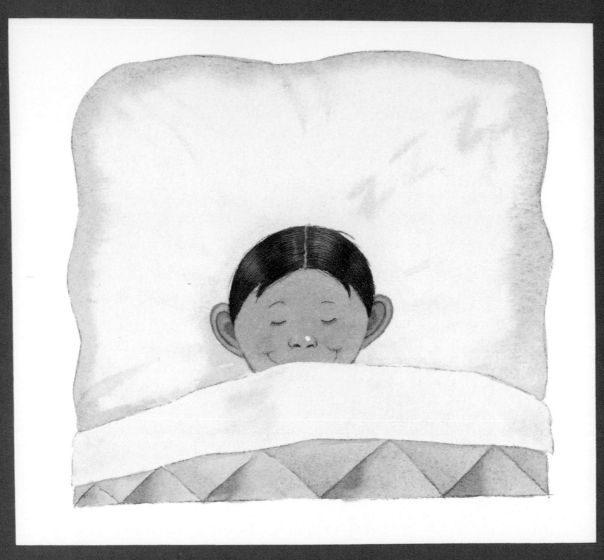

Billy told all his worries
to the worry dolls.
He slept like a log.

The next morning Billy went home.
That night he again told all his worries
to the dolls. He slept like a stone.

Billy slept well the next night,
and the night after that.

But the night after that, Billy started to **worry**.

He couldn't stop thinking about the dolls—
all those **worries** he'd given them....
It didn't seem fair.

The next day Billy
had an idea.
He spent all day
working at the kitchen
table. It was difficult.
At first he made lots of
mistakes. He had to
start again many times.

But finally Billy
produced something
very special . . .

some worry dolls for the worry dolls!

That night EVERYONE slept well—
Billy *and* all the worry dolls.

And, after that,
Billy didn't
worry very
much at
all.

And neither did
his friends....
Billy made worry dolls
for ALL of them.

Worry dolls, also known as trouble dolls, come from the Central American country of Guatemala. Legend has it that the dolls were created by a young Mayan sister and brother whose mother—a weaver of beautiful cloths—had fallen ill and was unable to produce cloth to sell at the market. The children decided to use their mother's scraps to make tiny dolls, which they put in pouches that they also made from the scraps. The daughter is said to have told her worries to a few of the dolls, only to awake the next morning feeling much less troubled. And when the children brought the dolls to the market the next day, they met a mysterious stranger with a tall hat who listened to the sister's story and then bought all the dolls. According to the story, when the girl got home, she found the dolls from the night before in her pocket, along with a note from the mysterious stranger instructing her to share one worry with each doll before placing them under her pillow at night.

To this day, children in Guatemala often trust their worry dolls to take away their worries as they sleep, and this custom has spread across the world.